PHONICS CHAPTER BOOK 3

ONCE UPON A HILL

An Appalachian Tale

by Wiley Blevins
Illustrated by Fian Arroyo

Scholastic Inc.

New York   Toronto   London   Auckland   Sydney

Copyright © 1998 by Scholastic Inc.
Scholastic Phonics Chapter Books in design is a trademark of Scholastic Inc.
All rights reserved. Published by Scholastic Inc.
Printed in the U.S.A.
ISBN 0-590-03080-9

1 2 3 4 5 6 7 8 9 10   14   04 03 02 01 00 99 98

Dear Teacher/Family Member,

Scholastic Phonics Chapter Books provide early readers with interesting stories in easy-to-manage chapters. The books in this series are controlled for sounds and common sight words. Once sounds and sight words have been introduced, they are repeated frequently to give children lots of reading practice and to build children's confidence. When children experience success in reading, they want to read more, and when they read more, they become better readers.

Phonics instruction teaches children the way words work and gives them the strategies they need to become fluent, independent readers. However, phonics can only be effective when reading is meaningful and children have the opportunity to read many different kinds of books. Scholastic Phonics Chapter Books cover many curricular areas and genres. They are carefully designed to help build good readers, but more importantly, to inspire children to love reading.

CONTENTS

Chapter   **Page**

1 Papaw Jake 4

2 Big Steve Sackett 9

3 Cinder-Elly 16

4 The Race 23

 Papaw Jake

Last year, I spent a lot of time with my Papaw Jake. We had as much fun as two pigs in a bucket of slop.

Papaw lived on a big hill. The hill was named Pine Hill because of all the pine trees. Life was mighty fine on Pine Hill. Mighty fine!

Each day, Papaw and I would get up at five o'clock. We liked to make eggs and pancakes. "I hate the mess you make," Mamaw always said.

Papaw let me put the pans on the stove and get the eggs from the henhouse. Then he cracked the eggs and mixed them up. I liked my eggs that way.

"How do you make pancakes?"
I asked Papaw.

"Well," Papaw said, as he wiped
his chin, "just add a cup of this and a
dash of that."

Yep, that's how he made them.
When he was finished, Papaw piled five
little pancakes on my plate. They tasted
just fine. He gave Mamaw five
pancakes, too.

"Do you like them?" I asked.

"Mine taste mighty fine!" she said.
"Mighty fine!"

We liked to sit on the porch while we ate. I liked to see the fog lift off the hill.

"If you sit still, you might see a fox," Papaw always said. "He might even come up and shake your hand."

"Boy, do I love this hill!" I said.

"I do, too!" Mamaw said with a smile.

While we sat, Papaw liked to tell tales. "This tale is fact, or my name isn't Papaw Jake," he always said. Then he would tell a big whopper!

"What a shame," Mamaw always said. "Telling the boy such tales!"

But each time I would ask for more!

The best tale was the one about Big Steve Sackett. He was some brave man. This is how Papaw told that tale.

2 Big Steve Sackett

Once upon a time, there lived a man named Big Steve Sackett. He was the bravest man on the hill. Big Steve could even out-run, out-jump, and out-yell a mad bobcat. When he spoke, the whole hill shook.

Many folks would ask Big Steve for help. Big Steve would jump at the call to help someone.

Then came the big rain. It rained for many weeks. The raindrops were as big as Mamaw's red-and-white snack plates.

The creek behind our home rose. It rose and rose and rose. Before long, the whole place looked like a lake. Some homes broke into small bits and washed away. Many folks left the hill.

Mrs. Eve lived down the hill with her five boys—Mike, Tom, Tim, Dave, and cute Little Billy Bob. The creek rose so much, I could just see the top of their home.

Mrs. Eve and her five boys—Mike,
Tom, Tim, Dave, and Little Billy Bob—
jumped on top of the roof. They waved
and yelled for help. There was nothing
I could do!

Then I saw it. My nose almost fell off from shock. Big Steve Sackett rode by on top of a great, big, white whale. He was yelling for Eve and her five boys—Mike, Tom, Tim, Dave, and Little Billy Bob—to sit down.

Then he grabbed nine black snakes swimming by. He tied the nine snakes end to end, to make a rope. He used that snake rope to save Mrs. Eve and her five boys—Mike, Tom, Tim, Dave, and Little Billy Bob. One by one, they held onto the snake rope as Steve dragged them onto the whale. They all gave Steve a big hug.

Steve then swam to the top of Pine Hill. The whole time, Mrs. Eve and her five boys—Mike, Tom, Tim, Dave, and Little Billy Bob—hung on. Little Billy Bob waved to the hound dogs, pigs, and old Mr. Pete as they swam by.

But the water just kept coming. So Big Steve dipped down to take a sip. Well, he sipped so hard, up came all that water. Then Big Steve spit it some ten miles away. That's how Lake Hope was made. And that's a fact, or my name isn't Papaw Jake.

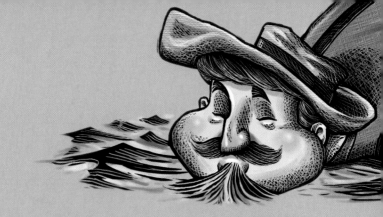

"Yikes!" I yelled. "Big Steve saved your home, too!"

"Yep," Papaw said, as he wiped his chin. "He saved all these homes on the hill."

"Tell me some other tale, Papaw. Please!"

"Well," said Papaw, "if you sit still, I'll tell you the tale of a gal named Elly."

Mamaw smiled. This was the tale she liked the best.

3 ⭐ Cinder-Elly

Once upon a time, there lived a gal named Elly. She was thin and had red hair. Elly was as nice and sweet as a glass of lemonade on a hot June day.

Elly had twin sisters named Grace Ann and Ginny Ann. Her sisters were as mean as two caged bobcats. They called her Cinder-Elly because her hands and dress were always black from those coal cinders she brushed out of the stove.

Cinder-Elly had just one dress, and it had been ripped twice. Grace Ann and Ginny Ann had nice orange and white dresses. The sisters didn't help Cinder-Elly. They just sat and ate while she did all the work.

One day, a note came to Cinder-Elly's home. On the last page it said that there was going to be a long race. The prize was a huge crate filled with gems and cash. "Golly!" said Cinder-Elly. "I don't have one red cent to my name. I just have to win that prize! Then I can get that nice dress down at Sam's Five-and-Dime shop."

But, Cinder-Elly had to ask her pa if she could run in the race.

"No," her pa said. "Your sisters Grace Ann and Ginny Ann can run in the race. You are too little."

Grace Ann and Ginny Ann just smiled.

"Who could help me?" Cinder-Elly sobbed. "I must win that race."

Just then, a strange woman came to Cinder-Elly's home. Her hair was as black as coal. Her dress was made of lace and looked fancy.

"Who are you?" Cinder-Elly asked.

"I am a friend," she said. "I can help you!"

"Do you want to win that race?"
the woman asked.

"Yes!" yelled Cinder-Elly. "I want it
more than a slice of my best lemon cake."

"Well," the woman said, "this is what I
will do. I will make a hat for you. This hat
will be like no other hat. I will also make
shoes for you. These shoes will be like
no other shoes."

You see, this woman could do strange
things. She could change a cat into a hat.
She could also change mice into shoes.

Cinder-Elly had a cute cat named Sage. The woman changed Sage into a hat and gave it to Cinder-Elly. The hat was so big it hid her face. "No one can tell who you are," the woman said.

She then made little red shoes from two mice. "If you put these on," she said, "you will run as fast as the wind."

21

Before the woman left, she gave Cinder-Elly a bit of advice. "When the race is finished, run home. At six o'clock your hat will change back into a cat. The shoes on your feet will change back into mice."

Just then, Papaw stopped telling the tale.

"Did she win the race?" I asked. "Did her hat change back into a cat?"

"Just sit still," Papaw said. "Soon you will see!"

4 ⭐ The Race

Papaw got a glass of iced tea and went on with the tale.

The day of the race came. Grace Ann and Ginny Ann smiled as they left home. "Have a nice day, Cinder-Elly," they said in a mean way. Cinder-Elly just waved and smiled back.

When they were down the hill, Cinder-Elly put on the hat the strange woman gave her. She put on the little red shoes, too. Like a jackrabbit, she snuck down to the place where the race would start.

Many kids from the hill were also there to race. They all sat by a big stage. On the stage were J.T. and his pa. Cinder-Elly liked J.T. He was the nicest boy on the hill. J.T.'s pa was the richest man in the state.

J.T.'s pa spoke about the race. He said the ten-mile race would go from the top of Pine Hill to Coal City. There would be one stop in the race. This stop would be at a place along Spice Creek. This was five miles away.

All the kids ran up to the starting line. Then J.T.'s pa yelled, "One, two, three . . . go!" The kids took off like mice chased by a cat. Some kids ran this way. Some kids ran that way. Soon they all ran the same way.

When they got to Spice Creek, many kids had to stop. Some quit the race.

"I feel sick," Grace Ann said, as she stopped. "I hate to run," Ginny Ann said, as she quit, too.

Cinder-Elly did not stop. She ran past them. Soon, she led the pack.

When she got close to Coal City, Cinder-Elly could hear the yells. "Go! Go! Go! Run like the wind! Speed up!"

"Who will win the race?" they yelled.

Cinder-Elly could see the finish line. But she felt a kid to her left. She also felt a kid to her right.

"I have to win this race!" she said. Just then, she tripped on a stone in the path. Her left shoe came off as she fell.

Cinder-Elly could hear the crowd yell, "Get up! Get up! Get up!"

She jumped up. And, with only one shoe, she ran as fast as she could.

Cinder-Elly crossed the finish line. "I win!" she yelled. "I win!"

Just as she said this, the huge clock struck six. Cinder-Elly's hat changed back into a cat. The shoe on her foot changed back into a mouse. Cinder-Elly ran home before anyone could see her.

She didn't even get her prize.

"Where is that fast gal?"
the folks asked.

"Where is she?" asked J.T.

There was no trace of Cinder-Elly.

J.T. picked up the shoe that
came off when Cinder-Elly fell.

"I will use the shoe to find her,"
he said.

J.T. went from home to home. "If the shoe fits, you will win the prize," he said.

Every gal on the hill put on the shoe. They all wanted that big prize. Grace Ann wanted the gems. Ginny Ann wanted the cash. When J.T. came to their home, they put on the shoe.

"I hope it will fit," Grace Ann said. But it did not.

"I hope it will fit," Ginny Ann said, too. But it did not.

J.T. was very sad. "Where is she?" he asked. "Where is that fast gal?"

Just then, J.T. saw Cinder-Elly. "Put this on," he said.

"She wasn't in the race," Grace Ann and Ginny Ann yelled. "Besides, she has work to do."

"Please, put it on," J.T. said.

Cinder-Elly smiled as she put her foot
in the shoe. It fit! Grace Ann and Ginny
Ann were shocked. "Golly!" they said.
"How can this be?"

J.T. was so happy. He gave the crate
of gems and cash to Cinder-Elly. She
used it to get that nice dress down at
Sam's Five-and-Dime shop. Cinder-Elly
was so happy, she gave some of the
gems and cash to her sisters.

Because of her kindness, J.T. fell in love with Cinder-Elly. Years after, she became his wife. All the folks on the hill came to see the big day. What a wedding it was!

J.T. and Cinder-Elly made a home on Pine Hill. They lived there as happy as two mice in a box of cheese. And that's a fact, or my name isn't Papaw Jake.

"Papaw," I asked, "isn't Mamaw's name Elly, too?"

"Yep," Papaw said.

"And, isn't your name Jake T. Sackett?"

"Yep," Papaw said, as he wiped his chin. "My name is J.T. Sackett, and my pa's name was Steve."

"Then were those tales fact?" I asked.

"Yep!" Papaw said with a wide grin.

Mamaw smiled, too. "Life on Pine Hill is mighty fine," she said. "Mighty fine!"

PHONICS

Decodable Words With the Phonic Elements

1

a-e	i-e
ate	fine
brave	five
gave	life
hate	like
Jake	mine
made	piled
make	Pine
name	smile
pancakes	time
plate	while
shake	wiped
shame	
tale	
taste	

2

e-e	o-e	u-e
Eve	broke	cute
Pete	home	used
Steve	Hope	
these	nose	
	rode	
	rope	
	rose	
	spoke	
	whole	

3

/j/g	/s/c
caged	advice
change	cent
gee	Cinder-Elly
gems	face
Ginny	fancy
huge	Grace
orange	lace
page	mice
Sage	nice
strange	race
	slice
	twice

4 review

a-e	i-e	u-e
came	Dime	huge
changed	fine	use
chased	five	**/j/g**
crate	iced	changed
gave	life	huge
Grace	like	gems
hate	line	Ginny
Jake	mice	stage
made	miles	strange
name	nice	**/s/c**
place	Pine	Cinder-Elly
race	prize	City
same	smiled	Grace
stage	Spice	iced
state	wide	mice
strange	wife	nice
tale	wiped	place
trace	**e-e**	race
waved	Steve	Spice
	o-e	trace
	close	
	home	
	hope	
	spoke	
	stone	
	those	